Twelve Days of Christmas

Illustrated by Susan Spellman

Published by Sequoia Children's Publishing,
a division of Phoenix International Publications, Inc.

8501 West Higgins Road
Chicago, Illinois 60631

59 Gloucester Place
London W1U 8JJ

Customer Service: cs@sequoiakidsbooks.com

www.sequoiakidsbooks.com

ISBN 978-1-6426-9137-5

On the first day of Christmas
my true love gave to me
A partridge in a pear tree.

On the second day of Christmas
my true love gave to me
Two turtle doves
And a partridge
in a pear tree.

On the third day of Christmas
my true love gave to me
Three French hens,
Two turtle doves,
And a partridge in a pear tree.

On the fourth day of Christmas
   my true love gave to me
Four calling birds,
Three French hens,
Two turtle doves,
And a partridge in a pear tree.

On the fifth day of Christmas
  my true love gave to me
Five golden rings,
Four calling birds,
Three French hens,
Two turtle doves,
And a partridge in a pear tree.

On the sixth day of Christmas
    my true love gave to me
Six geese a-laying,
Five golden rings,
Four calling birds,
Three French hens,
Two turtle doves,
And a partridge in a
    pear tree.

On the seventh day of Christmas
   my true love gave to me
Seven swans a-swimming,
Six geese a-laying,
Five golden rings,
Four calling birds,
Three French hens,
Two turtle doves,
And a partridge
in a pear tree.

On the eighth day of Christmas
    my true love gave to me
Eight maids a-milking,
Seven swans a-swimming,
Six geese a-laying,
Five golden rings,
Four calling birds,
Three French hens,
Two turtle doves,
And a partridge
in a pear tree.

On the ninth day of Christmas
    my true love gave to me
Nine ladies dancing,
Eight maids a-milking,
Seven swans a-swimming,
Six geese a-laying,
Five golden rings,
Four calling birds,
Three French hens,
Two turtle doves,
And a partridge
in a pear tree.

On the tenth day of Christmas
    my true love gave to me
Ten lords a-leaping,
Nine ladies dancing,
Eight maids a-milking,
Seven swans a-swimming,
Six geese a-laying,
Five golden rings,
Four calling birds,
Three French hens,
Two turtle doves,
And a partridge
in a pear tree.

On the eleventh day of Christmas
    my true love gave to me
Eleven pipers piping,
Ten lords a-leaping,
Nine ladies dancing,
Eight maids a-milking,
Seven swans a-swimming,
Six geese a-laying,
Five golden rings,
Four calling birds,
Three French hens,
Two turtle doves,
And a partridge in a pear tree.

On the twelfth day of Christmas
    my true love gave to me
Twelve drummers drumming,
Eleven pipers piping,
Ten lords a-leaping,
Nine ladies dancing,
Eight maids a-milking,
Seven swans a-swimming,
Six geese a-laying,
Five golden rings,
Four calling birds,
Three French hens,
Two turtle doves …

And a partridge in a pear tree!